Three Little Pigs

My First Reading Book

Story retold by Janet Brown
Illustrations by Ken Mortor

ARMADILLO

D1063885

Three little pigs are looking for adventure.

They wave goodbye to their friends and go out into the big, wide world.

What do the three little pigs hope to find in the big, wide world?

The first little pig meets a man carrying straw.

"May I have some straw to build a beautiful house?" he asks.

"Certainly, little pig," says the man.

The first little pig builds himself a straw house. Then he sits down for a nap.

What does the first little pig want to do with the straw?

Nearby lives a mean and hungry wolf. The wolf knocks on the door of the straw house.

"Little pig, little pig, let me come in!" he calls.

"Not by the hair of my chinny chin chin, will I open the door and let YOU come in!" cries the little pig.

"Then I'll huff and I'll puff and I'll blow your house down!" roars the wolf.

So he huffs and he puffs and the straw house falls down. The wolf runs inside and gobbles up the first little pig.

How does the wolf make the straw house fall down?

The second little pig meets a man carrying wood.

"May I have some wood to build a large house?" he asks.

"Certainly, little pig," says the man.

The second little pig builds himself a wooden house. Then he sits down for a nap.

What does the second little pig do after he has built his house?

Soon the wolf comes knocking on the door.

"Little pig, little pig, let me come in!" he calls.

"Not by the hair of my chinny chin chin, will I open the door and let YOU come in!" cries the little pig.

"Then I'll huff and I'll puff and I'll blow your house down!" roars the wolf.

So he huffs and he puffs and he HUFFS and he PUFFS and the wooden house falls down. The wolf runs inside and gobbles up the second little pig.

What does the wolf do when he has blown down the house?

The third little pig meets a man carrying bricks.

"Please may I have some bricks to build a strong house?" he asks.

"Certainly, little pig," says the man.

The third little pig builds himself a brick house. He works late into the night.

What kind of house does the third little pig want to build?

Soon the wolf comes knocking on the door.

"Little pig, little pig, let me come in!" he calls.

"Not by the hair of my chinny chin chin, will I open the door and let YOU come in!" cries the little pig.

"Then I'll huff and I'll puff and I'll blow your house down!" roars the wolf.

So he huffs and he puffs and he HUFFS and he PUFFS. Then he huffs and he puffs some more. But the brick house does not fall down!

Why do you think the third little pig's house doesn't fall down?

The next day the wolf returns.

"Little pig!" he says. "Let us go and dig turnips together tomorrow morning!"

The little pig goes to dig turnips that evening. When the wolf arrives in the morning, the field is empty and the little pig is at home eating turnip stew.

The wolf is very cross. But he says, "Little pig, let us go and pick apples together tomorrow morning!"

When the wolf arrives in the morning, the little pig is already up in the tree. "Here!" yells the little pig, and throws a juicy apple at the wolf. Then he jumps down, leaps into a barrel and rolls away down the hill to his brick house.

What does the third little pig throw at the wolf?

The wolf races after the little pig. He leaps up onto the roof of the brick house.

"I'll get you!" he roars, and climbs down the chimney.

But the little pig puts a pan of water onto the fire. The wolf falls down the chimney and into a large pot of water. The little pig slams the lid on to the pot, and nobody ever sees the greedy wolf again.

And the third little pig lives happily ever after in his brick house.

What happens to the wolf when he comes down the chimney?

Look carefully at both pictures.
There are five differences between them.
Can you spot them?

Answers:
1) Door on cottage
2) Mummy Pig's handkerchief
3) Bird on gate
4) Third little pig's handkerchief
5) Trees in the distance